PRESENTED BY

Lane Dunwoody

WESTMINSTER SCHOOLS

SMYTHE
GAMBRELL
LIBRARY

ASHLEY F.

THE FIVE SPARROWS

A JAPANESE FOLKTALE

ADAPTED BY
PATRICIA
MONTGOMERY
NEWTON

ATHENEUM   1982   NEW YORK

For my mother and father

27533

This story was adapted from *Anthology of Japanese Literature*,
compiled and edited by Donald Keene, published by Grove Press, Inc.

LIBRARY OF CONGRESS CATALOGING IN PUBLICATION DATA

Newton, Patricia Montgomery.
The five sparrows.

SUMMARY: When a kindly old woman is richly rewarded for nursing
a wounded sparrow back to health, a greedy neighbor attempts
to emulate the old woman and brings trouble upon herself
and her family.
[1. Folklore—Japan]   I. Title.
PZ8.1.N48Fi   398.2'4528883'0952   [E]   82-3881
ISBN 0-689-30936-8   AACR2

Text and Pictures copyright © 1982 by Patricia Montgomery Newton
All rights reserved
Published simultaneously in Canada by
McClelland & Stewart, Ltd.
Composition by Dix Type Inc., Syracuse, New York
Printed by Connecticut Printers, Bloomfield, Connecticut
Bound by Halliday Lithograph Corporation, West Hanover, Massachusetts
First Edition

A long time ago, in a place far to the east, an old woman sat outside her home winnowing rice for the evening meal. The spring morning was bright and beautiful, and as the old woman worked, she listened to children at play nearby.

The shrill cry of an alarmed bird made the old woman look up. Some of the children were throwing stones at the sparrows, who had flocked to eat her spilled grains of rice.

One of the stones had met its mark.

It had struck a lone sparrow and broken its back. The injured bird flapped and struggled helplessly as a crow swooped down, its sharp beak ready to kill the defenseless creature.

Horrified, the old woman ran toward the sparrow, clapping and shouting at the crow until she frightened it away. Then she tenderly picked up the terrified sparrow, calming it with soothing strokes.

The old woman found a small basket and carefully arranged a soft nest of cloth scraps, covered the basket, and left the bird to rest.

In the afternoon, she carried the basket into her house. There she had prepared a medicine of ground copper dust, which she lovingly fed the sparrow from a dropper made of twig.

Her family, who had gathered for the evening meal, laughed at her efforts to heal the wounded bird.

"Mother, haven't you better things

to do with your time than to waste it on a silly sparrow?" her daughter-in-law said. "That bird is too sick and stupid to even notice your fussing."

The old woman ignored her daughter-in-law's thoughtless words and the jests of the rest of the family and continued to care for the tiny bird.

Each day she fed it rice and water and medicine. After a few weeks, the sparrow began to hop about weakly.

Whenever she left the house, the old woman cautioned her family to look after the bird and give it food and fresh water. But they refused to help. "Why do you bother? It's only a sparrow," they said.

"I don't care what you think," replied the old woman. "It's such a helpless creature."

The sparrow's health continued to improve. And finally, after several months, it was able to fly.

One sunny day in early summer, the old woman knew the sparrow was ready to be set free.

Sadly, she stroked its tiny head one last time. Cupping the bird in her hand, she slid back the screen, opened her palm, and released the sparrow.

It faltered as it left the old woman's hand. Then it found its wings and flew to the top branch of a distant tree.

Each day thereafter the old woman searched among the sparrows that pecked through the dirt in front of her house for the one she had grown to love during the days and weeks of caring for it. She longed to hear its cheerful chirps once more.

She would sigh wistfully as she tossed a few grains of leftover rice for the birds, hoping one was her own.

Then one morning, the old woman heard a loud chirping at her

window. "Could that be my sparrow?" she wondered.

When she went to look, there it was. Lovingly she caressed its dear head, as it hopped onto her finger. But the bird simply dropped a seed into her palm and flew away.

"My little sparrow did not forget me," she thought as she looked at the seed.

Her daughter-in-law, who had been watching, laughed and said, "Now, mother, why are you getting all teary over a silly bird. And what will you do with a single gourd seed?"

"I will plant it, of course. And I will remember my little friend while I am tending the plant," she added, smiling.

The old woman watered the gourd plant each day, then carefully pulled any weeds and plucked off every beetle.

When autumn arrived, the single plant was burdened with many huge gourds. The old woman fed them to her family and shared them with all her neighbors. No matter how frequently she picked the gourds, there always seemed to be more than she could possibly use.

The old woman was happy, and her family, feasting on the gourds, wasn't laughing at her any more.

At last, when every family in the village had shared in the bounty of gourds, the old woman decided to dry the eight that remained to use as containers. She took them inside and hung them to dry.

A few months later, as the old woman sat by her window watching some sparrows, she remembered the gourds.

When she went to look at them they appeared to be quite dry. Marveling at their great weight as she cut them down, she thought, "I must be getting weak in my old age."

Carefully cutting away the top of the first gourd, the old woman was astounded to find that it was filled with white rice!

Her daughter-in-law, hearing the old woman's cries of amazement, ran in and said, "Mother, what has happened?"

The old woman, with great excitement, explained to her daughter-in-law that the gourd was filled with rice.

"Impossible," her daughter-in-law snorted. "You are getting old. You must have put that rice there yourself and forgotten."

Grabbing the knife, the daughter-in-law whacked the top from another

gourd—and out poured white rice!

Amazed at this miracle, she sliced off the tops of the other six gourds and found they were all filled with white rice.

"Surely my little sparrow friend must be responsible for this wondrous good fortune!" the old woman exclaimed.

"Mother, let's pour all of this rice into one large basket and store it," her daughter-in-law suggested.

The old woman watched her daughter-in-law pour the rice into a large storage basket and helped her push the basket into the corner.

The women then went to inspect the empty gourds. They gasped with astonishment when they found the gourds filled with rice again!

Though the two women spent the entire afternoon pouring rice from the gourds into storage baskets, there was no end to the rice. As soon as they emptied a gourd, more rice appeared.

Before long the old woman was very rich because of the never-ending supply of rice.

Next door to the old woman lived another old woman and her family. Envious of their newly rich neighbors, this family resented the fine new clothes the old woman and her family were wearing. And they certainly didn't like hearing the daughter-in-law's constant boasting.

"Listen," they said to their mother. "Our whole village knows that family became rich because the old woman

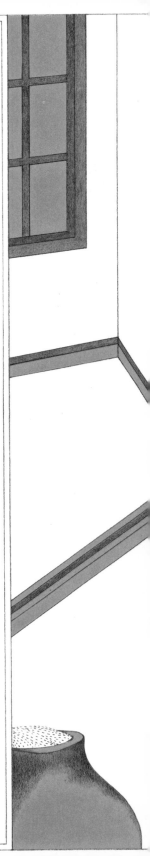

healed a wounded sparrow."

"Surely you are as clever as she," they continued. "If you were to find an injured bird and heal it, it would be equally grateful and would bring you a magic gourd seed too."

"Yes," agreed their mother. "You are quite right."

Thinking she would win the respect and devotion of her family (not to mention great wealth), the second old woman began to look for an injured sparrow. Although she spent the better part of each day watching the sparrows in front of her house, she never saw a wounded one.

After several weeks of watching, the old woman became angry and desperate.

"I could wait here until my daughter-in-law is as old and gray as I am and never find a wounded bird," she grumbled, kicking at a stone.

"Aha!" she declared triumphantly.

"That stone gives me an idea."

She bent over and picked up the stone. Taking careful aim, the old woman hurled the stone at a nearby group of sparrows.

"Hai-eee!!" she shouted, clapping her hands with glee. The stone had hit one of the sparrows, breaking its wing.

"How simple that was," she said to herself as she picked up the struggling bird.

"That other old woman became rich from healing only one sparrow. I would be much richer if I had three or four birds to tend."

After she put the injured sparrow into a basket, she threw some rice about to attract more sparrows.

Then she collected a pile of stones and waited for the sparrows to arrive. When at last the birds flocked to eat the rice, she began throwing stones. After a few unsuccessful attempts,

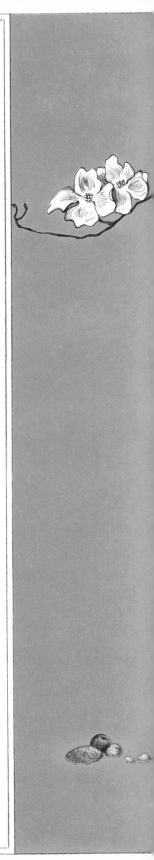

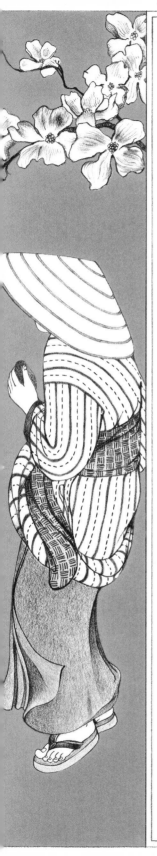

her aim improved and she hit three more sparrows.

She put the three sparrows into the basket with the first, took them home, and began giving them medicine, rice, and water. After several months of care, the four sparrows were healed.

The old woman released the birds, watching joyfully as they flew away. "Soon they will return with my seeds," she thought smugly.

"I will be even richer than my neighbors and my family will have great respect for me."

Several weeks later, the four sparrows returned. Each dropped a single gourd seed for the woman. Picking up the seeds, she grinned at the sparrows as they flew off. Then she planted the four seeds.

The old woman began preparations for the great amount of rice she expected from the quickly

sprouting gourd plants. She cleared out
a large space in the storage area of her
house and collected many baskets
and tubs.

Finally gourds began to form on
the plants. But they were few in
number and not very large.

"I will wait awhile before I pick
any gourds," she said. "These will get
larger and surely more will grow."

Her family was growing
impatient, however.

"Our neighbor had many large,
beautiful gourds to share with everyone
in our village," they reminded her.

"You had four seeds. There should be plenty of gourds for us and even more left over to share," they argued.

Not wanting to lose face with her family and neighbors, the old woman picked some of the gourds.

But the gourds smelled horrible. Anyone who tried to eat them got terribly sick. The villagers were extremely angry. They all marched over to the old woman's house,

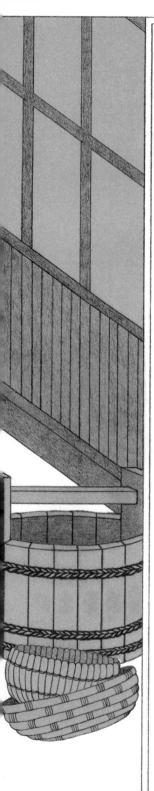

shaking their fists and shouting. But the old woman and her family were too sick from the poisonous gourds to take notice of their outraged neighbors.

Eventually the old woman's family recovered.

The old woman said to herself, "I probably picked those gourds too soon, which is why they made everyone so sick."

Now there were only a few gourds left. So she picked the remaining ones and hung them to dry, believing she would soon have an abundance of rice.

After a few months, the old woman was sure the gourds must be properly dried. She bustled about the storeroom, arranging all the baskets and tubs she had collected to hold the rice.

Whack! She chopped the top from the first gourd. When she turned it over to pour out the rice, however, she shrieked in horror.

Out flew thousands of flies!

Flies filled the house, swarming
and buzzing around the old woman
and her family, who came running
when they heard her screams.

Swatting at the flies with baskets
and rags, the family was finally driven
out of the house by the endless hoard
of hideous insects.

Amazed, the neighbors watched

as the old woman and her family ran
through the street surrounded by a
whirlwind of furious flies. The villagers
shook their heads in puzzled
amusement, watching the poor family
being chased up and down, around
and through and finally—out of the
village.

Several days passed before the old
woman and her family returned to their
home. It took another week for them to

rid the house of the remaining flies.

Next door the first old woman spread some rice in a winnowing basket for the sparrows. Five sparrows fluttered down.

As the old woman watched, she thought she saw them wink.